For Goldie girl and Ro —Jenny

◆

For Memere —Lisa

Center for Responsive Schools, Inc., is a not-for-profit educational organization.

© 2019 by Center for Responsive Schools, Inc.
All rights reserved. No part of this book may be reproduced in any form or by any electronic or mechanical means, including information storage and retrieval systems, without permission in writing from the publisher, except by a reviewer, who may quote brief passages in a review.

First edition, May 2019
10 9 8 7 6 5 4 3 2 1
Written by Jenny Rose
Illustrated by Lisa M. Griffin
Edited by Sera Rivers
Book design by Liz Brandenburg
Printed in the United States of America

ISBN: 978-1-892989-94-9
Library of Congress Control Number: 2018968250

Avenue A Books
An imprint of
Center for Responsive Schools, Inc.
85 Avenue A, P.O. Box 718
Turners Falls, MA 01376-0718

800-360-6332
avenueabooks.com
crslearn.org

Ready for Read Aloud

Jenny Rose ◊ Lisa M. Griffin

Rosa had a favorite book.

She read it to herself so many times,
she almost knew it by heart.

She carried it to school every day.

On Monday, when her teacher asked for read-aloud volunteers, Rosa wanted to raise her hand.

Instead, she shook her head no. She felt too shy!

"You'll feel ready soon. Practicing will help."

After school, Rosa read her book to a red ladybug.

The ladybug loved Rosa's reading so much, she fluttered her wings.

On Tuesday, the teacher asked again.

"Who would like to read aloud today?"

Today is...	
Monday	
Tuesday	X
Wednesday	
Thursday	
Friday	
Saturday	
Sunday	

Rosa wanted to raise her hand, but she still felt shy.

After school, Rosa read her book to a dappled green frog.

The frog loved Rosa's reading so much, he jumped high in the air.

After school, Rosa read her book to a fuzzy brown bunny.

The bunny loved Rosa's reading so much, she twitched her nose.

On Thursday, the teacher asked again.

"Who would like to read aloud today?"

Rosa wanted to raise her hand, but she still felt shy.

After school, Rosa read her book to a gray fox.

The fox loved Rosa's reading so much, he whished his tail.

After school, Rosa read her book to a freckled fawn.

The fawn loved Rosa's reading so much, she wiggled her ears.

On Saturday, Rosa read her book to a friendly garter snake, who flicked his tongue,

three silly squirrels, who scampered around a tree trunk,

and a nest full of baby robins, who cheeped and chirped!

Rosa felt a little less shy.

On Sunday, a boy peeked around the tree.

Who are you?

I'm Leo. I just moved in next door.

What are you reading?

"It's my favorite book.

Will you read your book to me, please?"

Rosa felt shy again when she thought about reading to a person.

But Leo smiled.

"I heard you reading to the animals. I know you can do it!"

Even though Rosa still felt a little shy, she decided to try.

She began reading, quietly at first,

then a little louder.

Her voice grew strong and steady, carrying in the breeze.

When she finished, she felt only a tiny bit shy.

On Monday morning, Rosa dressed for school and carefully tucked the book in her backpack.

She and Leo walked to school together.

When they got to their classroom, Leo stopped.

"I don't know anybody. I'm too shy to go in."

"You know me. We'll go in together.

I know you can do it!"

The teacher introduced Leo to the class. Rosa helped him find a seat.

And when the teacher asked...

"Who would like to read aloud today?"

...Rosa raised her hand.

Rosa walked toward the reading circle—and froze.

Suddenly, she felt as shy as before!

Rosa looked around the room. She saw a frog. She saw a ladybug. She remembered reading to all her animal friends.

Rosa took a deep breath and imagined...

Rosa still felt shy—but she felt ready for read aloud.

She opened her book and began reading, quietly at first, then louder.